# MY MOTHER'S GETTING MARRIED

## by Joan Drescher

Dial Books for Young Readers
New York

*Published by Dial Books for Young Readers*
A Division of NAL Penguin Inc.
2 Park Avenue
New York, New York 10016

Published simultaneously in Canada
by Fitzhenry & Whiteside Limited, Toronto
Copyright © 1986 by Joan Drescher
All rights reserved
Library of Congress Catalog Card Number: 84-18642
Printed in Hong Kong by South China Printing Co.
First Pied Piper Printing 1989
(b)
10 9 8 7 6 5 4 3 2 1

A Pied Piper Book is a registered trademark of
Dial Books for Young Readers,
a division of NAL Penguin Inc.,
® TM 1,163,686 and ® TM 1,054,312.

MY MOTHER'S GETTING MARRIED
is published in a hardcover edition by
Dial Books for Young Readers.
ISBN 0-8037-0604-9

The art for each picture consists of a black
ink, watercolor, and dye painting, which is
camera-separated and reproduced in full color.

To Kristin, whose mother really did get married.
And to Kevyn and Sean, who shared her experience with me.

**M**y mother's getting married.
The wedding is in two more weeks.
Everybody says, "Isn't that wonderful!"
Everybody but me, that is.
I think it stinks.

I like things the way they are—with just Mom and me.
I know sometimes she's too tired to cook. So I surprise her
with a picnic when she comes home from work.

Then we have supper at the beach.

On Saturdays Mom lets me stay up late.
We watch old movies on TV and make popcorn
and have chocolate ice cream. Mom lets me
lick the spoon and calls me Katydid.

She never calls me Katydid when Ben's around.

When she and Ben get married, I bet we'll eat
at seven o'clock every night.
She'll cook icky carrots and mashed potatoes.

And Saturday nights I'll probably have to stay with a sitter.
She and Ben will go out and leave me behind. The way
he kisses her—ugh—I can't stand it!

When I told my class that my mother was getting married, some of the kids laughed and the boys made stupid jokes. They already tease me about other things, like not being able to ride a two-wheeler. I sure don't need my mother getting married!

But Miss Tuck was just like all the other grown-ups. She got really excited. "How wonderful that you'll have a new father!" she said.
I told her things are fine with just Mom and me.

I guess Ben's okay once in a while. But when he marries
my mother, it means he'll be here all the time.
Sharing the bathroom will be awful. I'm not going
to let him see my kitty pajamas, that's for sure!

We'll even have to eat breakfast together. He'll probably
eat up all the Zoom Puffs. And he'll never go home
so it can be just Mom and me again.

I know Ben's trying to be my friend.
He's teaching me to ride my two-wheeler.
"Go for it, Katy!" he says. I go for it, all right!
I fall off the dumb bike and skin my knee.

Mom said I could invite anyone I wanted to the wedding. So I invited my whole class, even Miss Tuck. Ben bought me a new box of Magic Markers and I made some pretty nice invitations. But who wants to see my mother getting married? Nobody, I bet!

Only two more days until the wedding. Grandma and Grandpa are staying with us. But they're so busy getting the house ready that they don't even know I'm here. There's going to be a wedding cake with lots of layers. When I asked if it could be chocolate, they just said, "We'll see."

Grandma made me a flower girl dress.
I guess it's pretty but I wish I didn't have
to wear it to my mother's wedding.

Well, today's the day my mother's getting married. I think I'll just leave my blue jeans on under my flower girl dress.

I'm supposed to carry a basket and throw rose petals.
I'll throw them all right!

But, when Mom was getting married she
looked so happy, I decided to be good.
I threw the rose petals nicely and nobody
noticed my jeans.

The whole class came, even Miss Tuck,

and we had the best chocolate cake ever.

After the wedding party Mom threw her bouquet.
I caught it and everyone cheered.

But I felt really sad and angry when Mom and Ben were getting ready for their honeymoon. They could have taken me! Then Mom came up to say good-bye. "I hope you have a rotten time," I told her.

"What's the matter, Katy? What's wrong?"
"I don't want you to go away. I'm afraid
you'll love Ben more than me."
"But, Katy, I'll love you both more than ever!"

"Will we still have times together, just you and me?"

"Just you and me, and we can have fun with Ben too.

But no matter what, Katy,
you'll always be my Katydid."